Acting Edition

Late, A Cowboy Song

by Sarah Ruhl

I0589043

SAMUEL FRENCH

ISBN 978-0-573-70295-2

www.concordtheatricals.com
www.concordtheatricals.co.uk

FOR PRODUCTION INQUIRIES

UNITED STATES AND CANADA
info@concordtheatricals.com
1-866-979-0447

UNITED KINGDOM AND EUROPE
licensing@concordtheatricals.co.uk
020-7054-7298

Each title is subject to availability from Concord Theatricals Corp.,
depending upon country of performance. Please be aware that *LATE,
A COWBOY SONG* may not be licensed by Concord Theatricals Corp.
in your territory. Professional and amateur producers should contact
the nearest Concord Theatricals Corp. office or licensing partner to
verify availability.

This work is published by Samuel French, an imprint of Concord
Theatricals Corp.

No one shall make any changes in this title(s) for the purpose of production. No part of this book may be reproduced, stored in a retrieval system, scanned, uploaded, or transmitted in any form, by any means, now known or yet to be invented, including mechanical, electronic, digital, photocopying, recording, videotaping, or otherwise, without the prior written permission of the publisher. No one shall share this title(s), or any part of this title(s), through any social media or file hosting websites.

For all inquiries regarding motion picture, television, online/digital and other media rights, please contact Concord Theatricals Corp.

MUSIC AND THIRD-PARTY MATERIALS USE NOTE

Licensees are solely responsible for obtaining formal written permission from copyright owners to use copyrighted music and/or other copyrighted third-party materials (e.g. artworks, logos) in the performance of this play and are strongly cautioned to do so. If no such permission is obtained by the licensee, then the licensee must use only original music and materials that the licensee owns and controls. Licensees are solely responsible and liable for clearances of all third-party copyrighted materials, including without limitation music, and shall indemnify the copyright owners of the play(s) and their licensing agent, Concord Theatricals Corp., against any costs, expenses, losses and liabilities arising from the use of such copyrighted third-party materials by licensees. For music, please contact the appropriate music licensing authority in your territory for the rights to any incidental music.

IMPORTANT BILLING AND CREDIT REQUIREMENTS

If you have obtained performance rights to this title, please refer to your licensing agreement for important billing and credit requirements.

LATE, A COWBOY SONG was first produced by the Clubbed Thumb, at the Ohio Theater in New York City on April 21, 2003. The production was directed by Debbie Saivetz. The set design was by Andromache Chalfant, the lighting design was by Steve O'Shea, the costume design was by Eric Hall, the sound design was by Bray Poor, and the original music was composed by Michael Escamilla. The Production Stage Manager was Erin Cameron. The cast was as follows:

MARY.. Carla Harting
RED .... Addie Johnson
CRICK... Mather Zickel

LATE, A COWBOY SONG was subsequently produced by the Piven Theater Workshop in Evanston, Illinois on July 26, 2010. The production was directed by Jessica Thebus. The set design was by John Dalton, the lighting design was by JR Lederle, the costume design was by Janice Pytel, and the sound design was by Andre Pluess and Amy Warren. The Production Stage Manager was John Kearns. The cast was as follows:

MARY.. Polly Noonan
RED ....Kelli Simpkins
CRICK.. Lawrence Grimm

CHARACTERS

CRICK: Charming, fragile, and child-like.

MARY: Keeps her journal locked.

RED: She's no cowgirl, she's a cowboy.

Crick, Mary and Red need not be any particular race or ethnicity.

NOTES

Blue, the horse, and the painting exist as suggested, abstracted objects. Transitions should be fluid, without black-outs.

PLACE

A version of Pittsburgh.

A silhouette of a messy kitchen.

An image of the Marlboro Man hovers in the distance against blue light.

MUSIC

It would be nice if the actress playing Red could play the guitar. At the very least, she should be able to sing, accompanied by a live guitar. When Red sings, she ought to have a real cowboy outfit. Don't forget the chaps. The lyrics of the songs are mine. The music is up to you. (Or the music from earlier productions can be obtained.) Think simple iconic melodies. Yodling optional. Some melodies feel like honky-tok. Others – more like prayer under the night sky.

*To all the lady cowboys of heart and mind who ride outside
the city limits of convention, with special thanks to
Paula Vogel and Anne Fausto-Sterling*

PART ONE

1. You're late

A man – Crick – sits among dirty dishes.

A woman – Mary – steps in the door.

CRICK. You're late.

MARY. I know, I'm sorry.

CRICK. Where were you?

MARY. I ran into an old friend on the street.

CRICK. There's some food on the stove.

MARY. You cooked! Thanks.

CRICK. I love you, sugarplum.

They kiss.

MARY. I love you too. Smells good. What is it?

CRICK. Beef. Who'd you run into?

MARY. That girl we went to school with who always wore a money clip instead of carrying a purse.

CRICK. Oh, her. What's her name?

MARY. I haven't seen her in years.

CRICK. I didn't know you and her were friends.

MARY. Red. Red is her name.

CRICK. That's right. Red.

MARY. What's wrong with Red? I like her.

CRICK. She used to make jokes all the time that weren't funny.

MARY. I think she's funny.

CRICK. Maybe I have a better sense of humor than you do. Just kidding.

What did you do with – "Red"?

MARY. Had some coffee.

CRICK. Where?

MARY. What does it matter?

CRICK. I want to be able to imagine your day – every moment – like a beautiful detailed painting – the sort a Russian might paint on a hollow egg.

MARY. I don't think any Russians are interested in painting my life.

CRICK. Where'd you get coffee?

MARY. Green Shutters.

CRICK. You took her *there?*

A pause.

MARY. What's wrong with Green Shutters?

CRICK. You got coffee at a Chinese restaurant?

MARY. There are no other restaurants on that block.

CRICK. That's where *we* go.

MARY. I told you – there are no other restaurants –

CRICK. You were supposed to be home for dinner.

MARY. I know. I'm sorry. I should have called. Thanks for cooking.

She eats her food.

CRICK. I have a headache.

MARY. Oh – you do? I'm sorry. The one you get right there?

CRICK. Yes.

MARY. Do you want me to rub your head?

CRICK. Sure. Thanks.

She starts rubbing his head.

CRICK. Do you have any money?

MARY. Why?

CRICK. Can't you just answer the question – simply and elegantly – yes or no – in the same manner in which it was asked?

MARY. I have a little money.

CRICK. Can I have some?

MARY. What for?

CRICK. I just need it. Do you not trust me?

MARY. Of course I trust you.

She stops rubbing his head.

CRICK. Aw – why'd you stop?

MARY. Sorry.

CRICK. So you'll give me the money.

MARY. I just want to know what it's for.

CRICK. It's a surprise.

MARY. How much?

CRICK. Five hundred dollars.

MARY. Jesus.

CRICK. You don't have five hundred dollars? I thought you were an heiress.

MARY. I'm not an heiress.

CRICK. You're more of an heiress than me.

MARY. That's true. Most people are more of an heiress than you. They – like – inherit money from their jobs. Like a paycheck.

CRICK. Look – fuck you.

MARY. I don't like your language.

CRICK. In a just society people with more money give money to people with less money. I know you agree with that.

MARY. Yes – I do.

CRICK. If I had more money than you I'd give my money to you.

MARY. But you never do have more money than me.

CRICK. But I could.

MARY. Yes. You could. But you don't.

CRICK. You want to tally it up? See who's spent more on who? In the mind of God, who do you think has spent more money on who? Me or you?

MARY. Me.

CRICK. You think God cares? It's just money. It's not your soul. Money is meant to be spent.

MARY. Right.

CRICK. And I know you have five hundred dollars. Just sitting there. Doing nothing. Your soul should just sit there. Doing nothing. Not your money.

MARY. I'll write you a check.

CRICK. Thanks.

MARY. It's my whole savings.

CRICK. Don't worry, honey. I'll give it back to you. I'm just going borrow it.

How is whatserface, anyway?

MARY. Red?

CRICK. Yeah, Red. What kind of name is Red, anyway. Who does she think she is, the Marlboro Man?

MARY. She is, kind of. Red's a cowboy.

CRICK. Oh, yeah right – a cowboy in Pittsburgh.

MARY. She is – she wears a cowboy hat. She wore a big hat into the Green Shutters. It was kind of funny. People looked at her and she just tipped her hat. She does things to saddles and harnesses. She rides things. She can make a horse fall asleep – she sings horse lullabies for a job. She gets paid for it. She says it's beautiful, when a horse falls asleep. She says it's like if God fell asleep. Because God would sleep standing up – just in case he had to wake up – to take care of anything.

CRICK. It's cows that fall asleep standing up. Not horses.

MARY. Oh – I thought she said horses.

CRICK. Cows. Horses only fall asleep if they have to – if they're put in stalls. They should roam free. Don't you think.

MARY. It's nicer to think of horses falling asleep. I don't like to think of a cow falling asleep. It's not as pretty. Why is a cow not as pretty as a horse.

CRICK. People in India think cows are beautiful. They put cows in their art.

MARY. I don't know about that.

CRICK. What'd you talk about – you and *Red?*

MARY. I told you – horses falling asleep.

CRICK. Did she make a pass at you?

MARY. Yeah – I fucked her.

No, she didn't make a pass at me.

Jesus.

CRICK. What's wrong with you? Using language like that?

MARY. I'm going to my mother's house.

CRICK. You haven't eaten your dinner.

MARY. I'm not hungry.

CRICK. Why not? Hey – did you eat *dinner* with her at the Green Shutters?

MARY. No.

CRICK. The coffee – filled you up – all by itself?

MARY. Yes.

CRICK. Never known you to be satisfied by cream and sugar.

MARY. I didn't have cream or sugar in my coffee.

CRICK. Oh, you took it cowboy style. That's your new way, huh, tough girl?

MARY. Yeah. That's right. I don't like your tone of voice. I'm going to see my mother.

CRICK. You didn't finish your dinner.

MARY. I'll eat it later. I want to see my mother.

CRICK. Tell her I say hello.

MARY. I will.

Mary turns to go.

CRICK. Bye.

Crick looks pained.

Mary turns back.

MARY. I'm sorry.

CRICK. What for?

MARY. For being late.

CRICK. Don't go to your mother's. Stay here with me. We'll make up.

MARY. What do you mean: we'll make up?

CRICK. You know what I mean. We'll make up. Come here.

Crick pulls Mary to him.

They kiss.

2. Red

A woman – Red – in a cowboy hat –

leans against a tree and strums a cowboy tune on her guitar.

Stars and moon overhead.

She sings.

RED.
OH, AS THE SUN SETS
THE HORSES DO SLEEP
THE FIELDS THEY ARE LONG
AND THE CRICK IT IS DEEP...

OH, FIND ME A CHILD
WHO GROWS INTO A MAN
WHO CRIES LIKE A BIRD
AND FLIES LIKE A – CRAYON...

3. Summer

CRICK. You're late?

MARY. Yes.

CRICK. How late?

MARY. I think – I don't know – I wasn't keeping records...

CRICK. Don't you just know these things?

MARY. You're supposed to keep records. I used to keep records in my diary – I put a red mark – but I forgot.

CRICK. Mary.

MARY. Once when I was little –

CRICK. Should we take a test?

MARY. I don't want to. I'm scared of those tests.

CRICK. So we'll just wait and see.

MARY. I guess.

CRICK. What about when you were little?

MARY. I forget.

CRICK.	MARY.
Well, you know how I feel about it.	Oh, I remember. When I was little I put a red mark in my diary to keep track and someone saw my diary and asked what's that red mark for and I had to say that's when I have my period. And they passed my diary around the cafeteria.

CRICK. Oh, honey. That's horrible.

He kisses her on her forehead.

CRICK. No wonder you don't want to keep track.

MARY. I'm glad I'm grown up now.

She thinks about being grown up and starts crying.

CRICK. Aw honey, aw honey, aw honey, don't cry. It'll work out. We'll get married.

MARY. Oh, Crick.

CRICK. What kind of wedding do you want to have?

MARY. I don't know.

CRICK. Would you have bridesmaids?

MARY. Oh – I don't know –

CRICK. I think we shouldn't have bridesmaids. Those matching dresses – it's weird. Like seven nurses in lilac preparing to take you to your death-bed. I don't want to have a big party. Something small. Because it's between us, right?

MARY. Yes.

CRICK. It's about our love. I don't want people getting drunk and falling all over a dance floor. That's no way to celebrate our love.

MARY. You're right. I never thought of that.

CRICK. A lot of poetry and music and flowers. Love isn't pretty like that. They try to make it pretty. Like a funeral. Cover up what's really going on. With people in uniforms running around arranging things. And meat cooked all wrong. Love is between two people. It's not about acquaintances throwing up in the bathroom. I hate that.

MARY. I want *some* flowers at the wedding.

CRICK. You do? Aw, honey. What kind of flowers do you want?

MARY. Those little blue ones, like you find in a field.

CRICK. We'll have lots of those flowers, lots and lots and lots.

MARY. I think they're called forget-me-nots.

CRICK. I love it when you know stuff about plants.

We'll have forget-me-nots. A whole bundle. You'll carry some, I'll carry some. No music, okay? But we'll have a whole room of those little blue flowers. And some really good meat, cooked over a grill. We should get married soon.

MARY. Aw, Crick.

CRICK. Before you start to – show.

MARY. Oh –

CRICK. What do you want to name our kid?

MARY. I was thinking Jack?

CRICK. I never liked the name Jack.

Pause.

Mary looks pained.

CRICK. What's wrong?

MARY. I love the name Jack.

All my dead relations are named Jack.

CRICK. Oh, that's right. I'm sorry, honey.

Jack, it is. What do I care about a name! We're gonna have a baby!

Crick whirls Mary around the room.

CRICK. But it has to have my last name, okay?

MARY. Why?

CRICK. There're only three Thorndiggers left in the United States. Plenty of Smiths, no offense honey.

MARY. Maybe Smith could be the middle name.

A long pause.

MARY. Crick? Maybe Smith be the middle name.

CRICK. Hold on. I'm thinking. Jack Smith Thorndigger.

MARY. Jack Smith Thorndigger.

CRICK. Sounds like we're trying to belong to a country club, having a last name for a middle name. But if it's what you want – okay – I like it. I like it.

MARY. What'd you do with that five hundred dollars?

CRICK. It's a surprise.

I'm so happy. Are you happy?

MARY. Yes.

CRICK. You've made me the happiest man in the world, Mrs. Thorndigger. I hope we have a boy, don't you? If we have a girl and she wears those lavender mini-skirts and the boys chase her around I wouldn't be able to stand it. I'd have to follow her all around, to school and to parties, just to make sure boys weren't looking at her funny.

MARY. Hey –

CRICK. What?

MARY. You never asked me to marry you.

CRICK. Aw, honey.

MARY. I want you to ask.

He gets down on his knees.

CRICK. With eyes the size of tulips, and the most perfect nose in Pennsylvania, Mary Smith: we have loved each other since we were eight years old. Will you marry me?

MARY. Yes, I'll marry you – my dearest love.

CRICK. My beautiful Mary Thorndigger. I love you.

MARY. I love you too.

They kiss.

Crick buries his head in Mary's lap.

MARY. Honey – there's one thing.

CRICK. What is it darling?

MARY. If we have a baby, you gotta get a job.

CRICK. No problem. I'll get a job.

4. Crick gets a job

At the museum. A job interview.

CRICK. Because I've always wanted to be a museum guard.

Because I've always loved paintings.

Because I've always thought that paintings should be in a person's house and not in a museum.

Don't get me wrong. I *do* want paintings to be in a museum.

And I swear to protect them. I would never remove one. Or touch one.

I promise to guard them and uphold all the regulations.

I've always wanted to be a museum guard. My whole life long.

Because how could you really look at a painting and love it and understand it if you see it for five minutes – you've got to look at it the whole day long. Maybe for your whole life long.

I'll be the best museum guard you've ever seen. I will.

I'm going to have a baby. I'm going to be the best father and the best museum guard you ever seen.

A pause while the museum interviewer asks: why's your name Crick?

Oh, yeah, people are always asking me that.

My father named me after the creek I was conceived near. Sort of a funny name, I know.

I always wished I were named John or Mark or something like that.

My wife and I won't make the same mistake with our baby.

We're naming it Jill, if it's a girl.

My wife – she wanted to name it Blue – but I said no, honey – the kids at school will make fun of it. Our child should have a nice old-fashioned name out of the Bible like Jill.

A pause while the imaginary museum interviewer speaks.

Oh? Really? Maybe it's the translation I read.

A pause while the imaginary museum interviewer speaks.

Really? I do. Well, that's wonderful. Thank you. I can't wait to start.

5. At the Green Shutters

Red wears a cowboy hat. Mary looks pregnant.

Mary and Red, finishing a large bowl of soup for two people.

Two fortune cookies on the table.

MARY. I love this soup. I'm going to learn to make it at home. The clear soup – with vegetables – all bright and clear and separate in the broth. You know how in Cambpell's soup the vegetables get all mushed together?

RED. Yeah.

MARY. I like it when the vegetables are separate. So a carrot really looks like a carrot. I wonder how they do that. I'm going to learn to make it at home.

RED. You know – I hear there's even better Chinese food outside of Pittsburgh.

MARY. Where?

RED. Places like New York. San Francisco.

MARY. Oh! Have you been there?

RED. Nope. You know me – can't bring a horse into the city.

MARY. No.

RED. But I hear they have the best Chinese food there. And not just Chinese food. But Asian food more generally.

MARY. What do you mean?

RED. The cuisine of other countries in Asia. Not just China.

MARY. Oh!

RED. Vietnamese, Japanese, Korean…

MARY. What's the food from Vietnam like?

RED. Never had it.

MARY. Me neither. I bet there's a cook-book. Or show on T.V.

RED. They have everything on T.V.

MARY. Yeah.

I wonder if they feel bad, making food for us in America.

RED. Who?

MARY. The Vietnamese and the Koreans. After those wars. Why would they want to cook food for us, d'you think?

RED. Maybe they don't want to. Maybe it's for the money.

MARY. What exactly happened in those wars anyway? Who was fighting who?

RED. The north, the south. It's always the north and the south.

MARY. Maybe if people appreciated – *really* appreciated – the cuisines of other nations – they would say to themselves – my body has been nourished by this other country. I will be good to its citizens.

RED. Could be.

MARY. Well, I just don't know.

RED. About wars? How they begin and how they end?

MARY. Yeah.

RED. Me neither.

MARY. I wish I knew.

RED. Me too.

All I know is what a cowboy needs. Simple food. No fancy spices.

MARY. Sounds nice.

RED. See – I don't cook for other people. I cook for me. One soul, eating under the night sky.

MARY. Can a soul eat?

RED. I reckon so.

MARY. Me too.

A pause.

MARY. Well. We'd better have our fortune cookies. What time is it?

RED. I have no idea.

Mary looks at a clock.

MARY. I'm late.

That's all right.

You can't rush a fortune cookie.

It's – a ritual.

She opens her fortune cookie. She reads it. She is troubled.

MARY. Huh.

RED. What's wrong?

MARY. I keep getting the same fortune.

RED. What's that?

MARY. It says: your onion is someone else's water lily.

RED. What does that mean?

MARY. I don't know.

RED. You eat lots of onions?

MARY. Not many.

RED. Huh.

I hear sometimes pregnant ladies get a taste for onions.

MARY. No, not me. I don't know. Onions make you cry, I guess. Maybe Crick is my onion. And he'd be someone else's water lily.

RED. He ever hit you?

MARY. My husband?

RED. Yeah.

MARY. No.

Of course not.

He's so gentle, he wouldn't hurt a fly. Why do you ask?

RED. Because sometimes you talk about him – like you're afraid of him.

MARY. Afraid of Crick? Nah. That's silly.

RED. What's he make you cry about?

MARY. Oh, I don't know. Stuff. What's your fortune?

RED. Your smile is so lovely it makes everyone realize that the world is a beautiful place.

MARY. It's true.

RED. Aw.

(A pause. They look at each other.)

RED. So you got a name for the baby yet?

MARY. I want to name her – Blue – if it's a girl. I feel like it's a girl.

RED. That's a pretty name. Blue.

MARY. It's kind of after you.

RED. Really?

MARY. Yeah – after I ran into you – I thought about your name. I thought, I want this baby to be a real individual-type-person. Like Red is. So I thought I'd call her Blue.

RED. I'm flattered.

MARY. I hope you don't think that's weird. I mean, I know we don't know each other very well and all.

RED. No – no – I'm flattered. Maybe I'll baby-sit for her – it – the baby – sometimes. When it gets born.

MARY. Maybe. I don't know. Crick says he wants it to be just me, him, and the baby. He likes the family intimacy feeling. With the lamps all aglow. Like Swedish paintings, he says.

RED. I never seen a Swedish painting.

MARY. Me neither. Crick goes to museums.

RED. Maybe we'll take it for walks.

MARY. What?

RED. The baby.

MARY. Oh – yes. The baby!

RED. I could show it the stables, outside the city limits.

MARY. Oh! That sounds like heaven.

6. Red Sings a Song

RED.

EATIN' SOUP UNDER THE PITTSBURGH SKY
EATIN' SOUP LOOKING IN HER EYES
WHO AM I TO DESCRIBE SUCH FRAGILE* DELIGHTS
I'M A COWBOY FROM PENNSYLVANIA

SHARIN' OUR FORTUNES AND SHARIN' RICE
SHARIN' ONE TABLE AND SHARIN' ONE NIGHT
WHO AM I TO DESCRIBE SUCH FRAGILE* DELIGHTS
I'M A COWBOY FROM PENNSYLVANIA

Fragile (pronounced with a long "i")

7. Christmas Morning

Christmas music.

Crick rips open brown wrapping paper on a painting.

Crick and Mary see an abstract expressionist painting;

we see only a frame.

He leans it against the wall, reverent.

Crick and Mary look at the painting.

MARY. It's nice.

CRICK. Is that all?

MARY. How much was it?

CRICK. Never mind about that. Do you like it?

MARY. What do I do with it?

CRICK. What do you mean: what do I do with it?

MARY. I'm not used to presents like this.

CRICK. So?

MARY. What do I do with it?

CRICK. Look at it.

She looks at it.

MARY. Again and again?

CRICK. It's not like: again and again.

*Crick puts a chair in front of the painting. Mary sits
and looks at it.*

MARY. I know, but –

CRICK. It's good practice to just *look* at something. If Eve
had just looked at that apple instead of eaten it, we'd
all be better off. If all the bad things of the world were
paintings, and we just looked at 'em, we'd be better
off. It clears your head, just to look at something.
Don't you think?

MARY. But how many times, I wonder?

CRICK. What?

MARY. I mean, if you own your own painting, how many times a day should you look at it?

CRICK. As many times as you want.

They look at the painting.

CRICK. Doesn't it clear your head?

MARY. Yeah.

Mary stands in front of the painting, posing.

MARY. How long do you think you could just look at me, without kissing me?

CRICK. Not too long.

MARY. Try.

He looks at her for a while.

He kisses her.

CRICK. Merry Christmas, Mary.

MARY. Merry Christmas. I love the painting. I really do.

8. Crick looks at his Painting

Crick puts the painting on the wall.

He looks at it.

He puts it on a different wall.

He looks at it.

He puts it on the floor.

He looks at it.

He does a push-up over it and looks at it.

He rolls over on his back.

He holds the painting above him.

He looks at it.

He puts it on the ground beside him.

He curls up next to it.

He looks at it.

9. Mary Makes Soup

Mary's kitchen.

She thumbs through the Joy *of Cooking.*

Her excitement mounts as the process becomes more and more violent.

MARY. "Consommé: a clear soup."

There it is!

"A clear soup is supposed to be as bracing as a clear conscience."

How about that. I've thought the very same thing. I wonder who wrote this cook-book.

(She looks to see who wrote the cook-book.)

Never heard of her.

"About Clear Soups:

"Because so much valuable material and expert time goes into the making of clear soups and because they taste so delicious, most of us assume that they have high nutritional value."

Yes, I do.

"It disappoints us to have to tell you that, while they are unsurpassed as appetite stimulators, the experts give them an indifferent rating as food."

That can't be right.

"Instead of calling for things young and tender, remember that meat from aged animals and mature vegetables will be most flavorsome. *Bones are disjointed and crushed*; meat is trimmed of fat and cut up. Bones, especially marrow bones with *gelatinous extractives*, play an important role in stock.

"As the stock heats, quite a heavy scum rises to the surface. If a clear soup is wanted, push the scummy *abluvinious* crust to one side. Continue simmering. Again, push the scummy foam to one side.

Add lean ground beef, one egg white and crumpled shell, and *several uncooked fowl carcasses.* Beat these additions into the stock."

My God.

It's violent, isn't it?

Mary fills a pot with water and puts it on the stove.

10. Mary and Red, Outside the City Limits

Red eats soup out of a thermos.

RED. I think you've done it, Mary. Just like in the restaurant.

MARY. Really?

RED. Yep. Dee-licious. How'd you do it?

MARY. You don't want to know.

RED. Why?

MARY. It was ugly.

RED. Guess things have to get ugly before they get nice.

MARY. Yeah. Red. You're not afraid of what anyone thinks of you, are you?

RED. Nope. Not really.

MARY. How'd you get like that?

RED. I dunno.

MARY. Is it because your name is Red? I remember, in high school, you always wore these red velour pants. They were the ugliest things I'd ever seen.

RED. I loved those pants.

I wore 'em every day. I wore 'em until I wore the crotch clear out. And then I bought another pair.

Red laughs.

Mary laughs.

They laugh about nothing in particular.

Then they stop.

MARY. Lately – I can't decide simple things, like should I eat this potato chip or should I take a walk. So I ask myself questions in my head. I close my eyes and ask: should I take a walk? And the voice answers: Yes or No, and I think it's my own voice, but I'm not sure. Sometimes I think it's God's voice. But I've never been sure about God. So it must be my voice. Do you ever do that?

RED. Nope.

MARY. If you want to eat something, you eat it.

RED. I reckon so.

MARY. And if you want to take a walk, you take a walk.

RED. I do.

MARY. You don't think about it beforehand.

RED. Nope.

MARY. That's nice.

RED. I think about some things beforehand.

MARY. Like what?

RED. Never mind. Maybe you think about things too much, Mary. You should learn to ride a horse. When you're riding a horse, there's no time to think, should I jump over this fence or shouldn't I. All of a sudden you're just jumping over a fence. You know?

MARY. But life isn't like that. Life is –

RED. What?

MARY. I don't know. I'm afraid of horses.

11. New Year's Eve

Crick watches It's a Wonderful Life.

Mary enters.

FROM THE TELEVISION:

– A toast…to my big brother, George. the richest man in town!

The crowd breaks into cheering. People sing "Auld Lang Syne"

MARY. This is on again? This was just on.

CRICK. Shhh…I love this movie.

MARY. Don't you want to go to my mother's house? She's all alone.

CRICK. In a little bit. It's about to end.

Mary picks up the phone. She dials a number.

Crick turns up the volume.

MARY. Happy New Year! How's your leg? We're just watching a movie. No – we didn't feel like going out. Crick? You want to talk?

CRICK. Just a second! It's my favorite part.

MARY. He says Happy New Year. Okay, Mom, I love you too. Bye.

She dials another number.

MARY. Hello? Hi. Happy New Year! *(Pause.)*

With the horses?

CRICK. Who's that?

MARY. It's Red. Want to wish her a happy New Year?

CRICK. No.

MARY. Okay, you too, bye.

FROM THE TELEVISION:

– Look daddy. Teacher says, every time a bell rings an angel gets his wings.

– That's right, that's right.

They watch the movie. Crick is moved.

MARY. You crying Crick?

CRICK. A little bit.

12. A Journal Entry

Morning light.

Mary takes her journal out from under the couch.

She unlocks her journal.

MARY. *(to the audience)* January 1. New Year's Resolutions: One: Write in Journal Every Day. Two: Read books about how to be a good mother and how to improve your sex life. Three: Learn to ride a horse.

Thoughts for the day: Bad things could happen. Your heart could stop ticking inside your body. Your husband could drop dead and you could find him laying there, his face blue. A window could fall on you. Some people have defective hearts that just stop ticking. There's nothing you can do. I might have one of those hearts. I might drop dead at any moment. Some people spontaneously burst into flames. No warning. It's true. I saw it on television.

My life is not so bad. I read somewhere in a book: you have a right to be happy. Or was it: you have the right to pursue happiness. That's right. You have the right to chase happiness.

13. Red: A Song

RED.
> OH, THE SKY DOESN'T WORRY ME AT NIGHT
> OH, THE FLY DOESN'T WORRY ME IN FLIGHT
> MY HEAD DOESN'T WORRY ME
> MY HEART DOESN'T WORRY ME
> MY FOREHEAD HAS NO WORRY LINES AT ALL…

14. Crick and Mary go to the Museum

CRICK. We'll start at the beginning. With the Middle Ages.

MARY. I thought we were starting at the beginning.

CRICK. It's the beginning of Western art.

MARY. I was just kidding – get it?

CRICK. That's pretty good!

MARY. Thanks.

CRICK. Used to be they painted people flat.

Like this.

Do you like it?

MARY. Everyone looks so – sad –

with blood coming out everywhere.

And flat.

Like someone ran over the Virgin Mary with the great big machine they use to clean ice at a skating rink.

CRICK. Let's go to the next room. You'll like that better.

Modern art.

They look at a new set of paintings.

CRICK. Which one's your favorite?

MARY. I don't know yet.

CRICK. Well, pick your favorite inside your head and then I'll guess it.

MARY. That's a good game. Okay.

CRICK. You picked?

MARY. Yes.

CRICK. Is it that one?

MARY. No.

CRICK. That one?

MARY. No.

CRICK. That one was my favorite.

MARY. Why didn't you guess it first? You didn't think we'd have the same favorite?

CRICK. Aw, Mary. How about that one?

MARY. Nope.

CRICK. I'm stumped.

MARY. It's that one. The one of flowers.

CRICK. Really?

MARY. Yeah.

CRICK. That's not even a famous one.

MARY. It must be kind of famous. It got picked for a museum.

CRICK. I've never heard of the painter.

MARY. Do you like it?

CRICK. Your one?

MARY. Yeah. Do you think it's pretty?

(He pauses to look at it.)

CRICK. I don't like paintings of flowers. Usually. But I like this one. Yes. I definitely do.

It reminds me of you.

MARY. So your favorite is that one.

CRICK. Yes.

MARY. Huh.

CRICK. What – you don't like it?

MARY. No – it's just that…if I were painting that woman, I would make her arms longer. Her arms look – funny.

CRICK. Honey, it's on purpose. It's modern art. Things don't look the way they really look in life.

MARY. Oh.

CRICK. Now do you like it?

MARY. Is it supposed to be pretty? To make a woman look deformed like that?

CRICK. It's – making a statement.

MARY. My stomach hurts.

CRICK. Do you want me to rub it?

MARY. Not in the museum. People would stare.

CRICK. Do you want to see the Greek art? You might like that better. The women's arms will be the right size.

MARY. That might make me feel better.

CRICK. Or we could head over to contemporary art. You could see my favorite painting in the entire world.

MARY. What's it called?

CRICK. Untitled.

She doubles over in pain.

MARY. Oh!

CRICK. What is it?

MARY. I think I might be having the baby.

Oh!

Crick! Lay me on that bench. Oh!

CRICK. Hold it in, Mary! Hold it in! Oh, honey! Is there a doctor!

15. Mary on the phone at the hospital

MARY. Hi, Mom. It's a girl! Yeah. Just like I thought. When she came out of me Crick yelled: It's a boy! Because he saw the umbilical cord which was sort of big but then the doctor said no, that's the umbilical cord, you have yourself a girl.

So – something weird happened at the hospital. No, nothing like that. I haven't told anyone, okay? So don't act weird about it.

When I was holding the baby – a doctor came in and said to me:

There's something urgent.

We aren't sure if the baby's a boy or a girl.

Hold on. Just listen, Mom.

I said: what? How is that possible?

They said: it's sort of like a boy and a girl too.

There are some implications, they said. We're going to do a little surgery. No need to tell the baby. And then they did a little surgery. Crick got – upset. But the doctors said: everything will be fine.

So I guess it's a girl now. I don't know why they couldn't have left well enough alone.

It's beautiful, Mom. The baby.

(Pause while the mother asks a question.)

Oh, no, we don't have one yet.

I want to call her Blue.

16. A Song

Red sings a song on her guitar.

Mary cradles the baby.

RED.
WHO WILL CRADLE THE MOUSE TO SLEEP?
THE CAT WILL.
WHO WILL CRADLE THE SUN TO SLEEP?
THE MOON WILL.
WHO WILL CRADLE THE MOON TO SLEEP?
THE SKY WILL.
WHO WILL CRADLE THE SKY TO SLEEP?
THE COWBOYS WILL.
OH, WHO WILL CRADLE THE SKY TO SLEEP?
THE COWBOYS WILL.
THE COWBOYS WILL.

A horse walks across the stage.

Red gets on the horse and rides offstage.

A real horse would be nice.

An abstract approximation of the horse will do.

Intermission.

PART TWO

1.

Mary nurses the baby.

She and the baby are bathed in light, like a Swedish painting.

Crick watches them.

CRICK. Look at you. Beautiful. The two of you.

MARY. Aw, Crick.

CRICK. I'm gonna take your picture.

He arranges the lamplight around Mary's head.

He takes their picture.

Crick holds the camera out in front of him

and takes a picture of the three of them.

CRICK. Our little family.

They rest for a while

in the idea of being a family.

MARY. Crick.

CRICK. Yeah?

MARY. We gotta decide her name soon.

CRICK. Yeah. I know.

MARY. She'll grow up weird, if she doesn't have a name.

CRICK. I know. That's what I keep telling you, honey. But I'm not calling her Blue.

MARY. I'm not calling her Jill.

CRICK. So let's keep calling her baby.

MARY. The more I look at her the more she looks like her name is Blue. Like those blue flowers at our wedding – remember?

CRICK. Look, I'm not calling my child Blue Thorndigger! That's weird. I told you. Kids at school would make fun of her.

MARY. Well then I'll keep calling her Blue and you keep calling her Jill. That's all there is to it.

CRICK. She's going to get confused.

MARY. I'm with her more than you are. She'll get used to Blue.

CRICK. You're so fucking underhanded. Whispering names in the baby's ear. Like a spy for the Chinese government. You and your Chinese soup. (*Pause.*) Just kidding.

MARY. Not in front of the baby.

CRICK. Sorry.

MARY. She won't feel like herself if we call her Jill – she'll feel – off – she'll search and search for her real intended name – and then one day – I'll tell her – your real name is Blue – but by then she'll be *wrong*. Because everyone is named Jill. And she's not like everyone.

CRICK. No, she's not like everyone.

Things are going to be weird enough, without her having a weird name.

MARY. Things aren't going to be weird. Things are going to be – fine.

CRICK. Yeah.

Mary puts the baby in a bassinet.

Crick begins building a temporary sculpture out of household objects.

MARY. Crick. I want that five hundred dollars back.

CRICK. What? Why? We're married. We share everything now.

MARY. I want to buy a stroller for Blue.

CRICK. I bet you could get a used stroller for fifteen dollars at the Salvation Army. I'll give you fifteen dollars.

MARY. But I want that particular money. The five hundred dollars you borrowed from me.

CRICK. Why?

MARY. The baby's going to need a lot of things. I want my savings. Just in case.

CRICK. Mary. Our money is the same money now. The day we got married, our bodies became one body and our money became one big money. You can't tell it apart. Each separate bill of green is – conjoined – one to the other – like – blades of grass – made into one holy field.

MARY. That's beautiful, Crick.

CRICK. Besides, I invested it.

MARY. What?

CRICK. Yeah, I invested it.

MARY. How do you know how to invest anything?

CRICK. You calling me dumb?

MARY. No.

CRICK. I invested it. In the painting I bought for you.

MARY. That was five hundred dollars?

CRICK. It's an investment. One day that painter will be discovered, and we'll be rich.

MARY. Oh, no.

CRICK. You have to believe in invisible things, Mary, like investments. Your problem is you don't believe in money unless it's right in front of you. Imagine – the value of a painting can grow – invisibly. It's like a marriage, just sitting there, every year, growing in value, the longer you keep it. Until one day, you have a golden anniversary.

MARY. You idiot. Paintings don't make a person rich.

CRICK. Did you just call me an idiot?

MARY. I'm sorry. I didn't mean it.

He makes his hand into a fist at his side.

MARY. Don't hit me.

CRICK. I wasn't going to hit you. Are you crazy?

MARY. I don't know. Am I?

CRICK. Mary.

MARY. If you hit me I'll ride a horse out of town. I will.

CRICK. Mary. What is *wrong* with you?

I bought that painting for you.

2. The Stables. Outside the City Limits.

Red is teaching Mary to ride a horse.

It would be nice if it were a real horse.

If not, an abstract approximation of a horse will do.

RED. Wanna get up?

MARY. He's so – big.

RED. You gotta remember that horses are big old fraidy cats. They're flight animals.

MARY. I think I'm a flight animal.

RED. Nah – he doesn't see you that way.

MARY. You sure?

RED. Yeah. Now, gimme your foot…

One, two, three…swing your right leg over!

Red gives Mary a leg up.

MARY. Whoah!

RED. Hold the reigns!

You don't wanna get onto a horse and not hold the reigns.

That would be – unadvisable.

Mary takes hold of the reigns.

Are you ready for a ride?

MARY. Yes I am!

RED. Good.

MARY. Oh – but I have to pick up the baby from my mother's in an hour. Before Crick gets home from work.

RED. Don't worry. That's plenty of time. We can climb over that crick on the other side of the hill.

MARY. We're going to cross the water?

RED. You're gonna love it!

MARY. Won't the horse slip on the rocks?

RED. Nah. Don't be a fraidy cat, Mary.

He's the fraidy cat. *(gesturing to the horse)*

You gotta be brave. You're the cowboy.

MARY. I'm the cowboy.

RED. That's right. Show no fear.

MARY. No fear! All right! I'm gonna kick him! Sorry, horse! Here I go!

RED. You got it, Mary!

MARY. Are you following me?

RED. I'm right behind you.

In slow motion,

Mary swings her arm overhead

as she and her horse ride offstage.

MARY. Yeeeee – haaaa!

Cowboy music.

3. Veteran's Day

Mary comes home from riding a horse.

She gets out her journal.

She writes in her journal,

something secret and beautiful.

She makes up a metaphor.

She looks around to see if anyone's

overheard her metaphor.

Crick walks in.

She leaves her journal on the table.

She puts a magazine on top of it.

MARY. What are you doing home from work so early?

CRICK. It's Veteran's Day. I went to work and they sent me home.

MARY. Oh. Welcome home!

CRICK. Let's make love, honey, it's Veteran's day!

They embrace.

MARY. What's gotten into you?

CRICK. This morning I was out of deodorant so I put your deodorant on and I smelled like you all day and it turned me on to smell myself.

He kisses her.

Hey – are you wearing eye make-up?

(Mary is wearing eye make-up.)

MARY. No.

CRICK. You are. Did you go out today?

MARY. No.

CRICK. Why'd you put on eye make-up, to be home all day?

MARY. I told you, I'm not wearing eye make-up.

CRICK. Come here. Let me see. Is that eye-shadow?

MARY. No!

CRICK. Aw, Mary. Come here, you.

How often do I have a day off?

He kisses her.

He inspects her eyes for eye make-up.

He licks his finger and tries to remove the eye-shadow.

He embraces her on the couch.

4. A Song

RED.

THE STORY IS OLD
'BOUT A MAN AND A WOMAN
WITH HEARTS AS RED AS MINE

OH, HE GAVE HER A CACTUS
AND SHE BROKE HIS HE-ART
AND LEFT HIM IN THE ROAD
TO – O CRY – Y – Y

ARE YOU BLUE TONIGHT HONEY?
ARE YOU ALL BY YOUR LONESOME,
IS YOUR CACTUS DRY TONIGHT?

ARE YOU BLUE TONIGHT HONEY?
ARE YOU BLUE BY YOUR LONESOME,
DID YOUR CACTUS DRY UP AND DIE?

5. Veteran's Day: One Hour Later.

Mary and Crick sit on the sofa.

Their clothes are mussed.

MARY. What is Veteran's Day, anyway?

CRICK. It's for veterans.

MARY. There are – so many holidays these days.

CRICK. We've always had Veteran's Day.

MARY. Well it *seems* like a lot – they come – one after the other, like a flock of terrible birds.

CRICK. Huh?

MARY. *(on the verge of tears)* And you're supposed to be celebrating, but you don't understand what you're celebrating, and you don't know who made up veteran's day, you don't even understand the *word*.

CRICK. You don't know what a veteran is?

MARY. Sure I know what a veteran is. But Labor Day – I mean what the hell is that?

CRICK. It's for workers.

MARY. But – *why?*

CRICK. So they don't have to work.

MARY. Labor day sounds like they *are* working. It's stupid.

CRICK. I don't know what's gotten into you, Mary. It's not healthy, you staying home with the baby all day.

MARY. Well, I'm not going back to work!

CRICK. I wasn't suggesting that.

MARY. Then what were you suggesting?

(Pause.)

CRICK. I lost my job.

MARY. What?

CRICK. I got fired.

MARY. Why?

CRICK. I touched – a painting.

MARY. What?

CRICK. At the museum is this painting of just the color red and white. Red on top and white on the bottom. You look at it and you just want to cry your eyes out – you don't know why. I look at it all day. I watch the people go by. They look at the painting and they are unmoved. It's like they have plastic flowers for souls. Sometimes I stay late just to look at it. Today was its last day. Then it goes far away.

I had to touch it. The paint is so thick. An inch thick. Or more. I wasn't going to hurt it. I waited for a holiday. I turned off the alarm. And I touched it. There was another alarm I didn't know about. It kept ringing. People came running. And you know what? It was worth it. To touch the paint.

Pause.

MARY. How could you be so dumb?

CRICK. Don't call me that! Why'd you call me that?

Crick curls up in a ball and cries.

Mary comforts him.

MARY. I'm sorry. I didn't mean it.

She cradles him.

CRICK. What are we doing to do, Mary?

MARY. We'll get by.

When do you stop working?

CRICK. Today.

MARY. When do they stop paying you?

CRICK. Today.

We'll have more time at home together.

You, me, the baby. That'll be nice. Won't it?

MARY. Yeah. That'll be nice.

6. A Pasture Outside the Stables.

Mary and Red watch untamed colts in a field.

RED. You cold?

MARY. No, I'm fine.

Red gives Mary her denim jacket.

MARY. Thanks.

Red tips her hat.

MARY. So those are the little ones? What do you call 'em?

RED. Colts.

MARY. Colts. That's right. Look at that one.

RED. She's a nasty one. She'll take a while to break. Usually girls are quicker.

MARY. You ever broken a wild horse?

RED. Yeah.

MARY. How'd you do it?

RED. There are lots of ways.

MARY. But how do *you* do it?

RED. You really want to know?

MARY. Yeah.

RED. Okay. Well, horses are afraid to be alone. If they do something bad, you make them stay away from the group. When they start behaving again, you invite them back. You make 'em leave and come back, leave and come back, leave and –

MARY. Come back.

RED. Yeah. Every time they come back, they're more tame.

MARY. How do you make a horse leave?

RED. You stare at 'em funny – make 'em afraid.

MARY. Like this?

Mary stares at Red. Red laughs.

RED. Kinda.

MARY. Why does a horse come back?

RED. For some reason, they want to be close to the person who's chasing them.

MARY. Why?

RED. Once a horse loves you, he'll do anything for you.

MARY. How d'you make a horse love you?

RED. They just do.

MARY. You ever been in love – with a person?

RED. Naw. I'm not much for people.

MARY. Why?

RED. Always seemed – kind 'a mean – always talking – always trying to get up a hill or push someone down a hill. Horses are so damn smart. Nice too. You know any people who are nice and smart both?

Mary thinks.

RED. See?

RED. And horses – so quiet – in the night – their tails going – nothing more peaceful in the world. I tell you.

MARY. Yeah.

RED. You and Crick fell in love real early, huh? When your hearts were busting out of your overalls? What was it – in the second grade?

MARY. Yeah – it was second grade.

RED. How do you know if you love someone in the second grade?

MARY. Oh, we knew.

We have the same birthday.

It was – fate.

RED. Hey, Mary?

MARY. Yeah?

RED. Do you mind if we just sit and don't talk for a while? Sometimes I like just to sit and not to talk.

MARY. Sure. I'll try it, I guess.

They sit and don't talk. The sun sets. They watch it.

MARY. That's pretty.

Oh – sorry. We're not talking, are we?

RED. That's okay. You say whatever pops into your head.

The sun sets some more.

MARY. There's no shadow over any part of it.

RED. Huh?

MARY. With you – not talking.

RED. Aw, Mary.

MARY. Let's do it some more. The not talking. I like it.

Red nods.

The sun completely sets.

7. The Horse Ride to the Front Door

Crick waits for Mary to come home.

He looks at his watch.

He looks at the magazines on the coffee table.

He sees Mary's journal.

He looks at the cover.

He puts it down.

He picks it up.

He reads it.

He is disturbed.

He hears the sound of horse's hooves coming from outside.

He looks out the window.

He sees Mary riding up to the front door

on a horse.

Mary enters.

MARY. Hi.

CRICK. What the –

MARY. I got a ride.

CRICK. Yeah! I saw!

MARY. I got a ride home.

CRICK. Mary! Riding a horse to our *front* steps – as though that were a perfectly *natural* thing to do – JESUS GOD IN HEAVEN!

MARY. You'll wake the baby.

CRICK. So let's all wake up – you, me, the baby! Because Mary, the unexamined life is not worth living. I've had it with your antics.

MARY. I haven't done anything wrong.

CRICK. You're late!

He throws a pot against the wall.

MARY. I know. I'm sorry.

CRICK. I've been waiting for you since the second grade.

MARY. You have me.

CRICK. A woman who *respects* her husband does not ride a *horse* up to his front door with another *man* –

MARY. Woman –

CRICK. For all the neighbors to see!

Who was that?

MARY. Red.

CRICK. It looked like a man.

MARY. I told you. She's a cowboy.

CRICK. I read your journal.

MARY. You what?

CRICK. I read your journal.

MARY. How could you?

CRICK. I was home all day, waiting for you. I wondered what you were thinking about. I thought maybe there was something nice in it – about us.

MARY. Did you read the whole thing?

CRICK. No.

MARY. What parts?

CRICK. You were riding a horse.

MARY. When?

CRICK. On Veteran's Day. You said you were home all day. Why did you lie to me?

MARY. I don't know. I was afraid.

CRICK. Why would you be afraid of me? Have I ever hurt you?

MARY. No.

CRICK. So then why?

MARY. I don't know.

CRICK. All I ever asked of you was a little honesty!

He throws a loaf of bread against the wall.

She starts crying.

CRICK. Stop crying!

MARY. Why?

CRICK. I can't be mad at you if you're crying!

MARY. I'm sorry.

I'm going to my mother's.

CRICK. Don't go.

MARY. YOU READ MY JOURNAL!

CRICK. I'm sorry. That was bad of me.

MARY. You can't ever do that again.

CRICK. I won't. I promise. Mary, no one will ever love you as much as I love you.

I love you I love you I love you I love you I love you I love you.

Kissing her.

MARY. I love you too.

CRICK. You still leaving?

MARY. Yeah. I need to take a walk.

CRICK. Whaddya mean, a walk?

MARY. To my mother's.

CRICK. That's a seven hour walk.

MARY. Yeah.

Take care of Blue.

CRICK. What? When will you be back?

MARY. I don't know.

Good-bye.

She leaves, holding her journal.

CRICK. We were supposed to ride off into the sunset together, Mary. We were.

8. Red sings a song on her guitar

RED.

LEAVE, LEAVE, LEAVE WHILE YOU'RE ABLE
DON'T YOU HAVE AN OVERGROWN HEART
DON'T YOU HAVE AN OVERGROWN STABLE.

LEARN HOW TO RIDE
'FORE YOU LEARN HOW TO SPEAK
YOUR LEGS WILL BE STRONG
WHEN YOUR EAR IT IS WEAK

9. Thanksgiving

Crick watches It's a Wonderful Life, *holding the baby.*

FROM THE TELEVISION:

– Now you listen to me! I don't want any plastics! I don't want any ground floors, and I don't want to get married – ever – to anyone! You understand that? I want to do what I want to do. And you're...you're...

– Oh, Mary...Mary...

– George...George...George...

– Mary.

The phone rings.

CRICK. Hello? Oh, hi Mrs. Smith. Mom. No – she's not home. I thought she was with you. I don't know where she is. Probably outside the city limits. At the stables. She's learning to sleep standing up. Oh, just a joke. Well, Happy Thanksgiving to you too, Mrs. Smith. Okay, then. Uh – wait – you have any friends over for dinner?

Well, you could come over here if you want. I have ingredients for turkey sandwiches. No – it wouldn't be a bother at all. Okay, then. Bye now.

He turns off the television.

He starts preparing two turkey sandwiches, holding the baby.

CRICK. Alrighty, Jill. We're going to make some sandwiches. Are you Daddy's little girl? Aw, yes, yes you are. That's right, honey.

Mary walks in.

MARY. Crick?

CRICK. Mary.

MARY. Blue.

They embrace, as in the scene we just heard in It's a Wonderful Life.

The baby witnesses their reunion, stuck inside their embrace.

MARY. Oh, Crick.

CRICK. Oh, Mary, Mary, Mary...

CRICK. I want to kiss every inch of you.

I want to look at every inch of you.

MARY. Oh, Crick.

Mary takes the baby from Crick.

MARY. Oh, Blue. I missed you, honey.

Is she all right?

CRICK. I want to kiss your hands! And your feet.

And your stomach.

Put her down for a second.

Mary puts the baby down.

Crick devours Mary with kisses.

CRICK. That was the longest we've been apart since the second grade.

It was torture.

MARY. Kiss me like in the movies.

They kiss.

CRICK. You back for good?

MARY. Yeah.

CRICK. Oh, Mary.

MARY. Oh, Crick.

They embrace some more.

CRICK. Did you miss me?

MARY. Of course I did.

CRICK. Where were you?

MARY. My mother's.

CRICK. She just called.

She was wondering where you were.

MARY. I was walking.

CRICK. Just walking?

MARY. I couldn't eat, I couldn't sleep. So I walked. Home.

CRICK. Aw, honey. Do you remember when I first knew I loved you?

MARY. Tell me again.

CRICK. It was our eighth birthday. We were supposed to blow out the candles on our cupcakes at the same time. But you were so beautiful, I couldn't blow out my candles. I just kept looking at you.

MARY. Oh, Crick.

CRICK. Let's have cupcakes tonight, to celebrate.

MARY. Okay.

Crick moves to get ingredients for cupcakes. He stops.

CRICK. Mary?

MARY. Yeah.

CRICK. I don't want you seeing that cowboy anymore, okay?

MARY. Why?

CRICK. I want to live a harmonious life. No cowboys, no Indians, just you and me. What do you say?

MARY. She's my friend.

CRICK. But I'm your husband. That's more important than a friend. I need you to promise me.

A pause.

MARY. All right.

CRICK. So you're staying?

MARY. Yeah.

CRICK. Stick with me, honey. From now on, every day is going to be like a holiday!

PART THREE: THE HOLIDAYS

The following sequence builds in speed until it is faster than real time.

1. Birthday

Mary and Crick sing to the baby.

MARY	AND CRICK.
HAPPY BIRTHDAY TO YOU,	HAPPY BIRTHDAY TO YOU,
HAPPY BIRTHDAY TO YOU,	HAPPY BIRTHDAY TO YOU,
HAPPY BIRTHDAY DEAR BLUE	HAPPY BIRTHDAY DEAR JILL
HAPPY BIRTHDAY TO YOU.	HAPPY BIRTHDAY TO YOU.

2. St. Patrick's Day

CRICK. I brought home shamrock shakes from McDonalds's. For St. Patrick's Day.

MARY. Wow. They're green.

3. Birthday

MARY. Happy birthday, Crick.
CRICK. Happy birthday, Mary.
MARY. On the same day –
CRICK. Of the same month –
MARY. Of the same year –
CRICK. Your mother –
MARY. And your mother –
CRICK. holding us –
MARY. At the same time.
CRICK & MARY. Happy birthday.

4. Valentine's Day

CRICK. Happy Valentine's Day, honey.

MARY. Should we go to church?

CRICK. For Valentine's Day?

MARY. Isn't he a saint?

CRICK. Yeah.

MARY. We never go to church. Why don't we go to church?

CRICK. We're not religious.

MARY. Oh. Yeah.

5. Christmas

MARY. Christmas is early this year.

CRICK. Christmas is always the same day.

MARY. Isn't there a holiday that comes early? Depending on the month, or the Leap Year, or the moon?

CRICK. I don't know what you're thinking of.

Mary looks out the window.

MARY. It's snowing.

CRICK. *(Singing)*
I'M DREAMING OF A WHITE CHRISTMAS, JUST LIKE THE ONES I USED TO KNOW...
MAY YOUR DAYS BE MERRY AND BRIGHT!

MARY & CRICK.
AND MAY ALL YOUR CHRISTMASES BE WHITE...

MARY. I hope the firecrackers don't scare the baby.

6. Groundhog Day

CRICK. Happy Groundhog Day, Mary.
MARY. No shadow.

7. Halloween

Mary, looking out the window.

MARY. The trick-or-treaters never come to our house. I wish more children lived on this street.

CRICK. We could have another.

8. Fourth of July

Crick lights Mary's sparkler with his sparkler.

They wave their sparklers.

9. Anniversary

CRICK. Happy anniversary, Mary.

MARY. Merry birthday, Crick.

Merry or happy?

CRICK. Happy.

MARY. Merry or happy?

CRICK. Happy.

MARY. Have a –

Have a – holiday.

CRICK. Happy –

MARY. What?

CRICK. Happy.

MARY. What?

Have a –

The sound of the apple dropping in Times Square and crowds from television.

The volume is up high.

Crick shouts along with the television:

CRICK & CROWDS. Ten, nine, eight, seven, six...

MARY. *(shouting over the television)* New Year's is early this year.

CRICK. *(shouting over the television)* New Year's is always the same day.

Crick blows a sound-maker.

MARY. *(shouting over the television)* Can we turn it down?

CRICK & CROWDS. *(counting down)* FIVE FOUR THREE TWO ONE! HAPPY NEW YEAR!

A collision of holiday sounds. Horns, wedding bands, ho ho ho's, the sound of an Easter bunny, the sound of a groundhog, the sound of prayers.

10. Day after New Year's

Mary alone.

She throws out streamers, party hats, and three boxes of Kentucky Fried Chicken.

MARY. *(to herself)* I'm sick of holidays.

(to God)

I'm sick of holidays!

(to the world)

I'M

SICK

OF

FUCKING

HOLIDAYS!!!!!!!

She sits down, surprised at herself. She breathes.

PART FOUR

1. Mary calls her Mother for Guidance.

MARY. Mom? Hi, it's me. No, I'm fine. Mom, I was wondering. Did it ever happen to you, when you reached a certain age, that every day felt like a holiday? *(Pause.)* No, not in a good way. I mean – I have no – recollection of the normal days – in between the holidays. Do you think having children could do this to you? Oh, the baby's fine. No, she doesn't know she's part boy yet. It's not like that. *(Pause. The mother says: well, what is it like?)* I don't know what it's like. She's just a baby. Thanks, Mom. Bye.

Mary sings a lullaby to the baby.

Red plays the guitar, in the background, accompanying Mary.

MARY.

WHO WILL CRADLE THE SKY TO SLEEP?
THE COWBOYS WILL.
OH, WHO WILL CRADLE THE SKY TO SLEEP?
THE COWBOYS WILL.
THE COWBOYS WILL...

Red takes up the song.

RED & MARY.

OH, WHO WILL CRADLE THE SKY TO SLEEP?

RED.

THE COWBOYS WILL.
THE COWBOYS WILL...

73

2. A Journal Entry

Mary composes a journal entry.

MARY. *(to the audience)* Dear Blue,

I'm writing you a letter, just in case, on the occasion of your birthday. Because sometimes I have a premonition that my heart is going to stop ticking. I don't know why – it's a premonition.

I wanted you to know, Blue, if you grow up to be a woman, and one day you start feeling kind of funny – like maybe you're a woman, but maybe you're not, I want you to know that you're not crazy. You're smart. And it's hard to grow up. Nature is – mysterious.

If I die, and you're in charge of my funeral, I want there to be cowboys. And cowboy songs. I want to be buried outside the city limits. And I want there to be Chinese soup. Clear broth. So everyone leaves with a clear head.

Does any of this make sense, Blue? I don't know why I'm writing this. I'll laugh about it when I'm seventy-two.

Love,

Your mother,

Mary

She locks the journal.

3. Christmas

It's a Wonderful Life *is playing in the background.*

FROM THE TELEVISION:

– I owe everything to George Bailey.
Help him, dear father.

– Joseph, Jesus and Mary, help my friend Mr. Bailey.

– Help my son George, tonight.

– He never thinks about himself, God. That's why he's in trouble.

– George is a good guy. Give him a break, God.

– I love him, dear Lord.

Watch over him tonight.

– Please, God, something's the matter with Daddy.

Crick puts up Christmas decorations.

A crèche, stockings, lights.

Mary enters from the bedroom.

She watches Crick for a moment.

CRICK. I'll rewind the movie for you.

MARY. Okay.

CRICK. You wanna help me with the stockings?

MARY. Sure.

CRICK. We'll have some egg-nog, open stockings…how 'bout that?

MARY. Sounds nice.

CRICK. What's wrong?

MARY. Oh – it's nothing.

CRICK. I wrapped all the presents.

MARY. Thanks, honey. I'm sorry I – wasn't in the mood.

CRICK. I hid all of Jill's Santa presents. I wrapped the doll with special paper.

MARY. Aw, that's nice.

Crick.

CRICK. Yeah.

MARY. I've been thinking. Maybe we shouldn't give Blue so many girl presents.

CRICK. What do you mean?

MARY. The dolls, and the dresses.

CRICK. Why not?

MARY. Maybe we can get her some in-between presents.

CRICK. What do you mean?

MARY. Like some paints, or, I don't know, building blocks.

CRICK. Why?

MARY. Maybe we shouldn't – *make* her – like – girl things, you know? If she doesn't want to.

CRICK. But she is a girl.

MARY. Kind of.

CRICK. I'm not having this discussion on Christmas Eve.

MARY. Then when?

CRICK. Later.

MARY. She's not a baby anymore.

CRICK. I know. She's a little girl.

MARY. But why does she have to be one thing or another?

CRICK. Because sometimes in life, Mary, you have to choose. You can't live on a fence. I won't have my daughter living on a fence.

Pause.

MARY. I don't feel like celebrating Christmas this year.

CRICK. What?

MARY. I don't want to celebrate Christmas.

CRICK. Not celebrate Christmas?

MARY. That's right.

CRICK. How can you not celebrate Christmas?

MARY. You just – don't – do it.

CRICK. Mary.

MARY. I'm going to go for a walk.

CRICK. You're going out for a walk – on Christmas Eve.

MARY. I know it's not – the thing to do. I'm sorry.

CRICK. What is it that you *want?*

MARY. I just want – to be with time, as it moves along.

CRICK. Aren't you doing that?

MARY. No. Time is going too fast. I want it to stop.

CRICK. Aw, honey. I know how you feel.

MARY. You do?

CRICK. Yeah. When I want time to slow down, I look at a painting.

Come here. Let's look at the painting together.

They look at the painting.

He holds her.

She tries.

CRICK. Doesn't it clear your head?

MARY. It's not working. I'm sorry. I'm going to take a walk.

CRICK. When will you be back?

MARY. When will I be back?

CRICK. What TIME will you be back?

MARY. I have no idea.

CRICK. Mary, if you leave on Christmas Eve, things will never be the same.

MARY. I'll be back. Don't worry.

A pause. They look at each other.

She leaves.

He throws a wrapped present against the wall.

4. At the Green Shutters, Christmas Eve.

Red pours Mary another glass of wine.

They are both a little drunk.

MARY. I wish I had a present for you.

RED. That's okay.

MARY. I'm not celebrating this year. I didn't wrap any presents. Crick wrapped all the presents.

RED. I never wrap presents.

MARY. Never? How do you surprise people?

RED. I'm full of surprises.

MARY. I bet you are.

RED. I am.

Well. We forgot about our cookies.

They break open their fortune cookies.

MARY. What's yours?

RED. What's yours?

MARY. No, you first.

RED. Ladies first.

MARY. You're a lady.

RED. I'm no lady.

MARY. I guess you're not a lady like that.

RED. Nope.

MARY. You ever wonder about "ladies first"? I wonder about "ladies first".

RED. What do you wonder?

MARY. I mean: when a man says, ladies first, and opens the door and follows right behind you, I wonder if it's so he can look at your butt.

RED. Sounds about right.

MARY. I'd like to be a real lady. I'd like to always say the right thing – like – if someone dies – a real lady says the right thing. She wears the right clothes to the wake – she doesn't stand out but she looks nice – with appropriate shoes – and she writes the right thing on stationary to the bereaved person. She writes something that makes them feel like carrying on with their life. No words crossed out or misspelled. She has a clear mind and a clear heart. Clear – like soup.

RED. I think *you* are a real lady.

MARY. No, I'm not.

RED. You are.

MARY. No, I don't wear the right things. I don't write the best thank-you letters and death-notes. I know I don't.

RED. Well, I think you're a true lady.

MARY. Well, thank you.

RED. See? A true lady knows how to accept a compliment.

MARY. I just did that, didn't I?

RED. Yeah.

(gesturing to the fortune cookies)

So. Like I said: ladies first.

MARY. Okay.

Mary opens it.

She is forlorn.

MARY. It's blank.

RED. Blank! That's terrible.

Let's get you another one.

MARY. No, no, don't bother.

RED. *(to an unseen waitress)* Excuse me, ma'am, my friend here – she got a blank fortune cookie. Would it trouble you greatly – to give us another one, please?
Thank you.
See? That wasn't so bad.

MARY. I'm embarrassed.

RED. Don't be embarrassed. It's your fortune – you paid for it.
Now. Open it.

Mary opens her second fortune cookie. It's blank again.

MARY. Oh…

RED. What is it? What's it say?

MARY. It's blank again.

(She is on the verge of tears.)

Oh, Red, am I going to die?

RED. Now, honey.

Don't cry.

These must be defective.

MARY. Well what does yours say?

RED. Mine, don't worry about mine.

MARY. But they're not all defective. Yours has a fortune.

RED. Let's see here. Mine says:

a family is a thousand blessings.

MARY. Oh! I'm going to die, aren't I?

RED. Now, listen. I don't have a family. Our fortunes got mixed up. You were s'posed to get mine, and I was s'posed to get yours.

Mary stops crying a little.

MARY. Do you think so?

RED. I know so.

MARY. But I don't want you to have a blank one.

RED. To me – a blank fortune is…an open sky on the horizon. Fill in the blank. A fortune no one's ever written up ahead of time, because no one could imagine a life as strange and as beautiful as the horse you're about to jump on.

MARY. That's beautiful.

RED. Should we blow this pop-stand?

MARY. Yeah.

RED. Now you're really late.

MARY. I don't care.

5. Outside the city limits

The same night, towards morning.

Red, Mary, and a horse in silhouette.

MARY. I've never seen anything like it. Those factories look like big magical tin soup cans. With light coming out the sides. I never knew factories could look so beautiful.

Red. Do you think it's possible for two people to experience time at the exact same speed?

RED. Yes I do.

MARY. How do you know?

RED. Try me.

MARY. What do you mean?

RED. *(in low tones.)* Mary.

(Pause.)

RED. Here. I'll show you. Dance with me.

MARY. I can't dance.

They dance

RED. Just a two step.

There, that's it.

They dance.

MARY. I'm late.

RED. There's no such thing as late. *Slow down.*

They dance.

MARY. Are we in horse time now?

RED. Yeah.

MARY. No one's late in horse time, are they?

RED. No.

They dance.

6. You're Late.

The same morning.

Crick is at the door, holding a baseball bat, very still.

Mary walks in the door.

CRICK. You're late.

She notices that Crick is holding a baseball bat.

MARY. What are you doing?

CRICK. Nothing.

Where were you? *Riding a horse?*

MARY. Yeah.

CRICK. All I ever asked from you was a little honesty!

They breathe.

MARY. Where'd you get that baseball bat?

CRICK. The basement.

MARY. What are you going to do with it?

Are you going to kill me?

ARE YOU GOING TO KILL ME?

CRICK. I just want to talk.

MARY. Okay, let's talk. Put down the baseball bat.

He does.

CRICK. Okay. Jill and I had a nice Christmas Eve. Did you have a nice Christmas Eve?

MARY. Yeah.

CRICK. Mary, I don't think you have a soul. You don't have any feelings. You just DO things. You're more like an animal. An ape, or a dog, or a horse.

MARY. I didn't do anything wrong.

CRICK. You lied to me. Let's make love.

MARY. Now?

CRICK. Yeah.

MARY. I don't want to.

CRICK. Why?

MARY. I just don't.

CRICK. Let's go in the bedroom. C'mon.

He tries to kiss her.

She winces.

He puts his hands on the back of her neck, hard.

MARY. Why are you putting your hands on my neck?

CRICK. I don't know.

MARY. TAKE YOUR HANDS OFF ME.

He takes his hands off her.

CRICK. You really don't love me, do you?

MARY. That's beside the point.

Blue enters.

The audience doesn't see her.

Crick and Mary follow Blue with their eyes. A silence.

CRICK. Well, look, honey. You're up just in time for Christmas breakfast. We're going to fry up some eggs and put on some bacon and then open stockings. What do you say?

Blue says nothing.

MARY. Take my hand, Blue. We're going on a walk.

Mary holds out her hand to Blue.

The imaginary Blue goes to her mother.

Mary turns to Crick.

MARY. And yes, I do love you. Good-bye.

Mary exits, with Blue.

7. Coda

Mary and Red in a vast landscape,

like the end of a cowboy movie.

Red wears a cowboy hat.

Red reaches into the stroller and pulls out another cowboy hat.

She puts it on Mary's head.

Crick looks at his painting.

He carries the empty frame

to the edge of a vast landscape.

He holds it in the air,

framing a field of color.

He tilts the frame, crooked.

RED & MARY. *(singing)*
OH, AS THE SUN SETS
THE HORSES DO SLEEP
THE FIELDS THEY ARE LONG
AND THE CRICK IT IS DEEP...

OH, FIND ME A CHILD
WHO GROWS INTO A GIRL
WHO RIDES LIKE A MAN –
WITH A MASK.

Lights down.

The End

www.ingramcontent.com/pod-product-compliance
Lightning Source LLC
Chambersburg PA
CBHW071929130726
47909CB00014B/2826